By the King's crown!

It is time to be a Knight - and do it right!

M

MIKE

D1349449

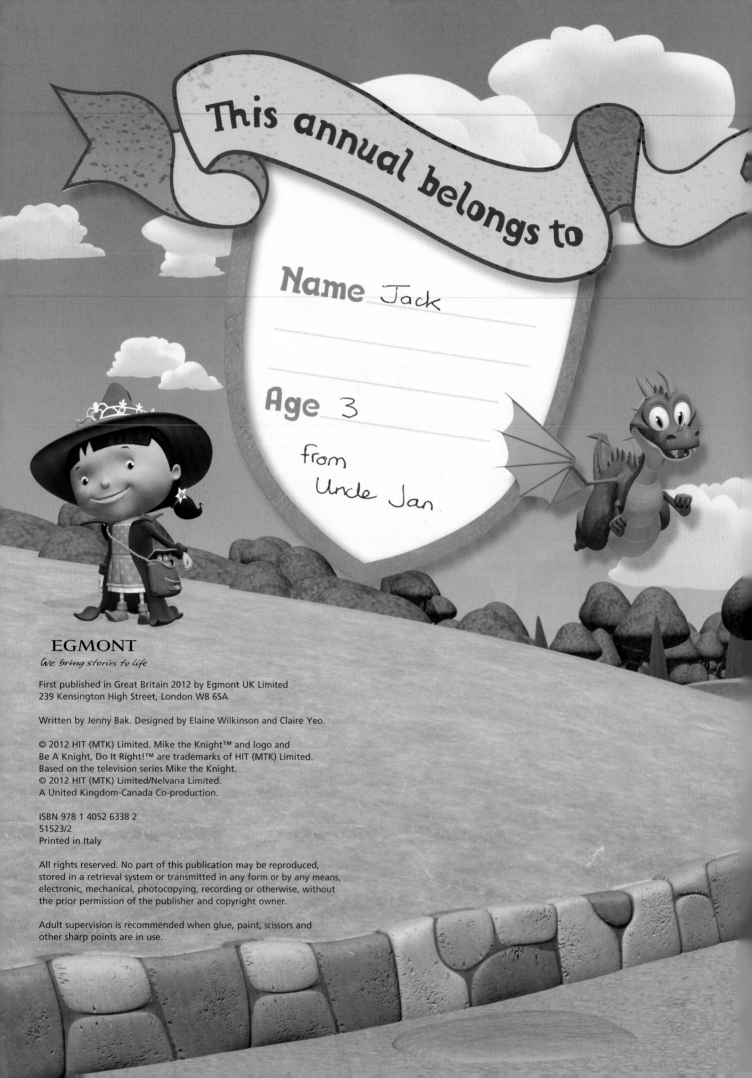

This annual belongs to

Name Jack

Age 3

from
Uncle Jan

EGMONT
We bring stories to life

First published in Great Britain 2012 by Egmont UK Limited
239 Kensington High Street, London W8 6SA

Written by Jenny Bak. Designed by Elaine Wilkinson and Claire Yeo.

© 2012 HIT (MTK) Limited. Mike the Knight™ and logo and
Be A Knight, Do It Right!™ are trademarks of HIT (MTK) Limited.
Based on the television series Mike the Knight.
© 2012 HIT (MTK) Limited/Nelvana Limited.
A United Kingdom-Canada Co-production.

ISBN 978 1 4052 6338 2
51523/2
Printed in Italy

Contents

All answers on page 68-69.

Hear ye, Hear ye!

Meet Mike the Knight, the bravest knight around!
His knightly missions take him all over town.

With help from his friends, Mike trains as a knight.
If there's a mission to do, he'll do it right!

We're so glad you're here
to play with young Mike.
We'll do puzzles and games,
and whatever you like!

Mike the Knight

Be a Knight, Do It Right!

The faraway Kingdom of Glendragon has a new hero ...

Mike the Knight!

To train as a knight, Mike goes on fun missions with the help of his friends.

Mike is **brave** and **bold**, **cheerful** and **cheeky**. All he wants is to be a real **knight**, just like his dad!

The Big Book for Little Knights-in-Training shows Mike everything he needs to be a great knight!

Put a tick next to the items Mike needs, and put a cross next to the ones he doesn't.

jam tart

shield

frog

guitar

helmet

sword

9

The Kingdom of Glendragon

Glendragon is a busy village with lots going on!

Whether Mike is on a **mission** to find yummy jam tarts or new shoes for Galahad, he can find **anything** he needs in the market square.

Glendragon Castle is where Mike lives with his family and friends. With his father, the **King**, away on important quests, his mum rules the kingdom.

Queen Martha is wise and caring, and often inspires Mike's knightly missions. Her two corgis are named **Yip** and **Yap**, because that's what they like to do! Can you spot them in the picture? Find a green frog, too!

Galahad

Brave and dependable, Galahad is **always ready** to join in Mike's knightly missions. Even though Galahad is a horse, he and Mike **understand** each other very well!

Galahad is very **handsome**, and he knows it! He likes to admire his many trophies ... as well as his reflection in the mirror.

When starting a mission, Mike goes down a slide from his bedroom to Galahad's stable.

Help him through the maze, being careful to avoid the hazards along the way.

Medieval Match

1

Draw lines to match Mike and his friends to their shadows.

2

3

4

5

a

b

c

d

e

Odd Knight Out

One of these pictures of Mike is different from the rest. Can you spot the odd one out?

1

2

3

4

5

6

Evie

Mike's sister Evie is a **wizard**-in-training. Though Evie tries hard to get her **magic spells** right, they sometimes go very **wrong**!

Evie has a big **book** of spells and a pet frog named **Mr Cuddles** to help her practise her magic training. She likes to tag along on Mike's missions, even when he doesn't want her help!

Potion Puzzle

Evie's workshop is in the big tree next to the castle. She keeps lots of colourful potions for her magic spells.

How many orange potion bottles can you see?

How many green potion bottles can you see?

Evie's next spell needs 8 potion bottles. How many more bottles should she fetch?

Spot the Difference

These two pictures look the same, but there are six differences in picture 2. Can you spot them all? Colour in a shield for each one you find.

Knight-in-Training

Once **upon a time**, in the Kingdom of Glendragon, Queen Martha had a special surprise for Mike. "It's a **postcard** from your dad!" she said. "He wants to know how your horse training is going."

"It's going well, Mum!" said Mike.

Queen Martha smiled. "Why don't you show me this afternoon? Then I'll write back to tell your dad all about it."

Mike was eager to show off how good he was. "By the King's crown, I'm Mike the Knight and my mission is to be the **best** horse trainer in all of Glendragon!" He pulled out his sword, but it had turned into a golden **goblet**, thanks to one of his sister Evie's wonky spells.

"And we'll help!" said Sparkie and Squirt.

Mike wanted Galahad to look his best, so he went with his friends to Hairy Harry's, the blacksmith. Harry had lots of **splendid** things for horses to wear.

Mike found **bells** for Galahad's ankles,
a fancy **saddle** with flags poking out and a big, floppy
feather for the horse helmet. Galahad didn't like them at all,
but Mike was too excited to notice.

Mike wanted to practise a bit before Queen Martha turned
up. The first task was **Silent Sneaking**. Evie put her frog,
Mr Cuddles, in the arena. Mike and Galahad were to
sneak up on him without being heard. But the bells round
Galahad's ankles
jingled and
jangled whenever
he took a step! Mr
Cuddles heard them
and hopped away.

"Try **Great Galloping** next," said Evie.

Mike guided Galahad around some poles in the Arena. But the flags on the new saddle got **caught** on the poles, making Galahad nearly fall over. The horse training was not going well!

"The last task is **Tricky Trotting**," called Sparkie and Squirt. This one couldn't go as badly as the others!

Galahad began trotting around the Arena. But the big feather **flopped** over his eyes, making it hard to see. Then it **tickled** his nose, making him give a great big sneeze!

"Ah-CHOO!" sneezed Galahad, and he fell into a heap on the ground along with Mike! Sparkie and Squirt ran over to help them up.

"What's wrong, Galahad?" asked Mike. "You did the tasks perfectly before."

Galahad blew the feather out of his eyes and shook the bells round his ankles **crossly**. Then Mike understood.

"I'm sorry, Galahad. I'm not a very good horse trainer, because I didn't **listen** to you," said Mike. "I'll take all these silly things off you now."

Evie and the dragons helped Mike take off the bells and the feather, then put on Galahad's regular saddle. Just then, Queen Martha arrived and sat in her throne in the Arena.

"Here's our chance to show Mum how good we are," Mike told Galahad. **"I'll be a knight and do it right!"**

Without the bothersome things, Galahad did the Silent Sneaking, Great Galloping and Tricky Trotting **perfectly**! Queen Martha and Evie clapped in delight.

"Your father will be so pleased when he learns how **knightly** you are. I wish I had a trophy to give you," said the Queen.

Mike pulled out his sword, which was still a golden goblet. "How's this, Mum?"

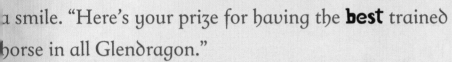

Queen Martha took the goblet, then handed it back to Mike with a smile. "Here's your prize for having the **best** trained horse in all Glendragon."

"Huzzah!" cheered Sparkie and Squirt.

Galahad snorted proudly as Mike patted him and said, "That's right, Galahad. You're **great** just as you are!"

The End

Sparkie

Sparkie is a **big** dragon and one of Mike's best friends. He can breathe **fire**, which helps in his job as the **cook** at Glendragon Castle. Sparkie is always happy to join in Mike's knightly missions, as long as they don't make him late for tea!

Sparkie is making a delicious lunch for Queen Martha. Circle the things that he can cook, and put a cross over the things that he can't cook.

Squirt

Squirt is a **little** dragon who gets scared easily, but is always ready to help his friends. He can spray **water** from his mouth, which is a big help when Sparkie accidentally starts a fire! Squirt can **fly**, and likes to make friends with the birds he meets in the sky.

Oh no, Squirt needs to put out the fire on these barrels! Can you help? Using a blue crayon, draw a stream of water starting from Squirt's mouth and finishing at the fire.

29

B e a Knight ...

Starting at number 1, join the dots to finish this picture of Mike the Knight, then colour it in.

Do It Right!

There are three things wrong with this picture of Mike, Sparkie and Squirt. Colour in a shield as you spot them.

Make a Knight's Shield

Ask an adult to help you make a knight's shield, just like Mike's!

What You'll Need:

- Large piece of cardboard
- Safety scissors
- Sticky tape
- Blue and red paint
- Paintbrush
- Glue
- Thick cord

① Cut a shield shape out of the cardboard.

②

Stick the tape along the edges of the shield to cover them from the paint.

3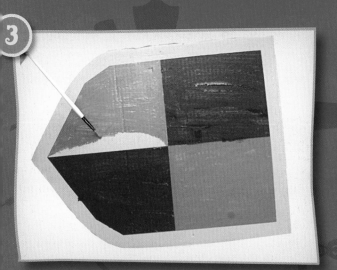

Paint the middle of the shield red and blue.

4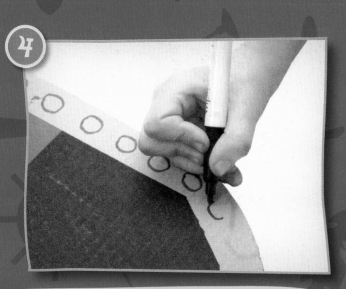

Remove the tape, then draw small circles around the edge of the shield.

5

Poke a hole either side of the shield, leaving at least 2cm from the edges. Cut a piece of cord long enough to tie through each hole, leaving a bit of slack to use as a handle.

Turn the page for help on putting Mike's symbols on your shield!

Just Like Mike

Mike has four symbols on his shield. Here's how you can put the same symbols on your shield!

With a pencil, trace these four shapes onto white paper. Cut out the shapes, then colour them in if you like. Glue them onto your shield, using Mike's shield as a guide.

Horseshoe Hunt

Galahad has lost his four horseshoes!
Can you find them in this picture?

36

Shield Shuffle

Queen Martha is sorting out the decorations that hang on the walls of Glendragon Castle. Draw and colour in the flag or shield that comes next in each row.

Which piece is missing from the jigsaw picture of Yip and Yap?

a   b   c

Sword Spell

Evie has enchanted Mike's sword to turn into odd things that later become useful for his missions. Today, he needs to build a birdhouse. Which sword would help Mike build it?

39

Troll Family

The Troll family live in the **Maze Caves** outside Glendragon. The villagers are scared of the trolls, but Mike knows that they're a very **friendly** family. Pa Troll is big and **strong**, Ma Troll bakes delicious **cakes**, and Trollee is one of Mike's best **mates**!

Maze Cave Maze

It's easy to get lost in the Maze Caves! Help Mike find his way to Trollee's home.

Piecrust Puzzler

Mrs Piecrust runs the bakery in Glendragon Village. Draw lines to match the pairs of yummy things she has baked.

The Vikings

Glendragon is often visited by three **merry** Vikings from a far-off land – Grey Beard, Broken Horn and No Beard. They cause **mischief** by **bouncing** all around the village and **taking** things that don't belong to them! But Mike always puts everything right, then sends the Vikings on their way home.

No Beard

Grey Beard

Broken Horn

43

Great Gallop

You can help read this story. Listen to the words and when you come to a picture, say the name.

Mike　　**Sparkie**　　**Squirt**　　**Vikings**　　**jam tarts**

It was Great Gallop Day, and  was very excited!

According to an old Glendragon tradition, he and Galahad

had to quickly gallop down to the river and leave a sack of

there. When they galloped back, the whole

village would celebrate by eating even more .

  went with and  to fetch

a big sack of from Mrs Piecrust.

Then, with everyone cheering them on,

and his friends started the Great Gallop to the river.

 wanted to be the fastest Great Galloper,

even faster than his dad!

But as Galahad raced down the road, the

began falling out of the sack!  asked,

"Shouldn't we stop to pick them up?" But  said,

"No, that would slow us down. Let's go faster!"

When they got to the river,  looked in the sack.

All the had fallen out! He didn't know what

to do, so he just left the empty sack on the riverbank.

When the friends returned to the village, Mrs Piecrust

handed out lots of  . Queen Martha said,

"Well done,  . You've saved us!"

was worried. "Saved us from who?" he asked.

"  !" shouted  in fear.

Three noisy  ran into the village and

began stealing the from the villagers!

The  came to the Glendragon river every

year to collect the sack of , but today they

found the sack empty. So they came to the village to

look for some, and were causing a big mess! Then,

 had an idea. He took the very last of the

 and put them on a machine that could

throw things very far. When the  went to

eat the  , Mike made the machine throw

the and the all the way to

the river! They cheerfully climbed into their boat

and sailed away with their tasty pastries. With the

village safe, everyone was happy again. Especially

when Mrs Piecrust brought out more yummy

 for all!

The End

Canine Count

How many pictures of Yip and Yap can you count?
Write the number in the box.

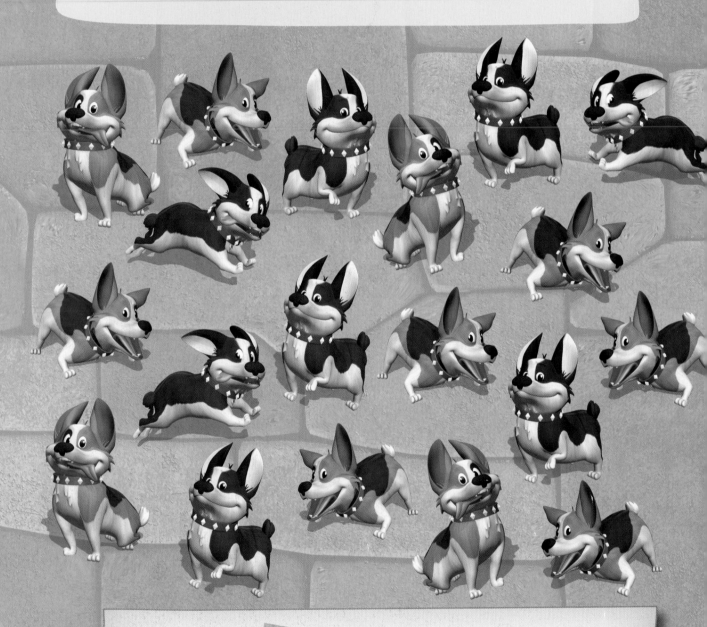

There are [ ] pictures of Yip and Yap.

Close Call

Which of the close-ups below can't be found in the big picture?

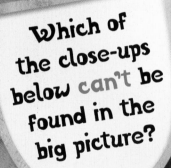

a

b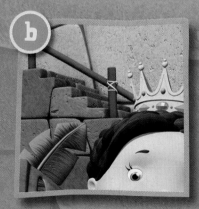

c

Bake Jam Tarts

Ask an adult to help you make these tasty jam tarts!

You Will Need:

- Tart or muffin pan
- Readymade rolled shortcrust pastry
- Butter
- Jam or marmalade

1

Preheat oven to 180 degrees or gas mark 4. Roll out the shortcrust to a thickness of just under a £1 coin.

2

3

Cut out circles using a wide cup or pastry cutter. Then grease a tart pan with a bit of butter.

Tuck the circles into the tart pan and add small spoonfuls of jam.

4

Bake the tarts for 15 minutes or until golden brown.

Let the tarts cool completely before eating ... jam stays hot for a long time!

The Buried Treasure

One day, Mike was training Galahad in the Arena. He looked up and saw a colourful **rainbow** in the sky.

"Whoa, look at all those colours!" shouted Mike.

"It's a rainbow!" gasped Squirt. "I've never seen a **real** one before."

Sparkie was surprised. "But that means you've never been to any of my **Rainbow Parties!** We'll have one just for you, with my special rainbow cupcakes."

Squirt spun excited circles in the air. "Special cupcakes for me? **Mmm!**"

There's a lot to do, and we don't have much time. Rainbows don't stay for long," said Sparkie.

Then we'd better hurry," Mike told the dragons. **"Come on!"**

On the way back to the castle, the friends met Trollee on the path.

"Hi, Trollee! Isn't the rainbow nice?" called Mike.

"Yes, and it's nice to find **treasure** at the end of the rainbow, too," Trollee replied.

"Treasure? Knights love treasure!" Mike thought for a moment, then gasped. "By the King's crown, that's it! I'm Mike the Knight, and my **mission** is to find the treasure at the end of the rainbow!"

"Have you forgotten about the Rainbow Party?" asked Sparkie worriedly.

But Mike was already looking to see where the rainbow ended. "We'll have the party after we've found the treasure," he shouted as he started Galahad galloping.

After Mike changed into his knightly armour, he pulled out his sword — but it had turned into a **kite**, thanks to one of Evie's spells! Evie joined them in following the rainbow's end to the centre of Glendragon Village. But when they reached the village, the rainbow had moved.

"There it is," said Evie, pointing towards the **Maze Caves**. Sure enough, the rainbow now ended near the caves where Trollee lived with his family.

"But what about the Rainbow Party?" asked Squirt.

"We have plenty of time," insisted Mike. **"Let's go!"**

Mike, Evie and the dragons collected some spades, then hurried to the Maze Caves. They found Ma and Pa Troll hanging their laundry on a clothesline, but they didn't find the rainbow. It had moved again.

"There, over the **Tall Tree Woods**," shouted Mike. He wheeled Galahad towards it.

"Mike, I need time to bake cupcakes for the Rainbow Party," said Sparkie.

"Don't worry, Sparkie. This won't take long," Mike laughed.

At last, Mike and the others found the **end** of the rainbow! They dug in the ground where it ended until their spades knocked against something. They pulled hard and out came ...

"A silver statue? A throne made of gold?" panted Mike, pulling as hard as he could.

"A giant turnip!" said someone nearby. It was Trollee! "Turnips are troll treasure. Ma Troll bakes the greatest cakes with turnips."

"A turnip?" Mike was disappointed. Then he caught sight of Squirt. The little dragon was trying to hang onto the fading colours of the rainbow, but there was nothing to hold. The rainbow was **gone**!

Sparkie and Squirt were very sad. They had missed their chance for the Rainbow Party.

"I'm really **sorry**," Mike said. "I know you wanted rainbow cupcakes." Suddenly, he smiled, "Maybe it's not too late!"

He ran back to the Maze Caves, with his friends following close behind. Evie had stayed there, doing **magic spells** for Ma and Pa Troll. She had changed all their laundry to bright rainbow colours, as well as the nearby rocks. Her last spell landed on Mike's giant turnip and turned it rainbow-coloured, too! He gave the turnip to Ma Troll and asked her to bake a cake with it.

"But we **can't** have a Rainbow Party without a rainbow," said Squirt, shaking his head sadly.

"It's time to **be a knight and do it right!**" said Mike. He asked Pa Troll to borrow the laundry, then pulled out his sword-kite. He tied the clothesline to the kite and flew it in the air. The brightly coloured laundry hung in the sky, **just** like a rainbow!

Then Ma Troll came out of the caves with a lovely rainbow-coloured cake.

"Huzzah!" everyone cheered.

'Thank you for making my Rainbow Party so special, Mike," said Squirt.

'You're welcome," smiled Mike. 'Next time there's a rainbow, he only **treasure** I'll look for s a rainbow **cupcake!**"

The End

Tails and Ladders

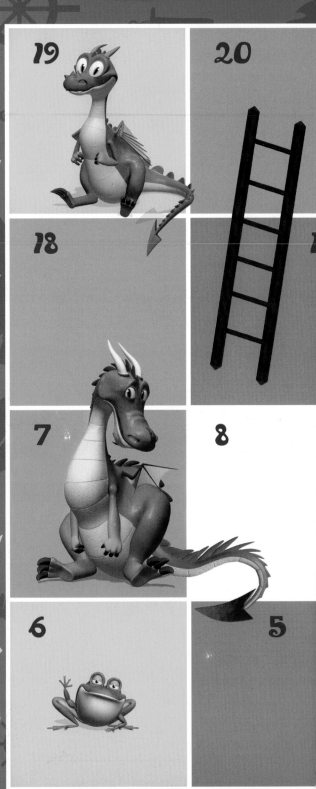

How to play:

✒ Place the counter on the start square.

✒ Take it in turns to roll the dice, moving across the grid row by row.

✒ If you land on a space with the bottom of a ladder, climb the ladder to the square at the top. But if you land on a space with a dragon, slide down its tail to the square at the bottom.

✒ The first player to reach the last square wins the Golden Helmet!

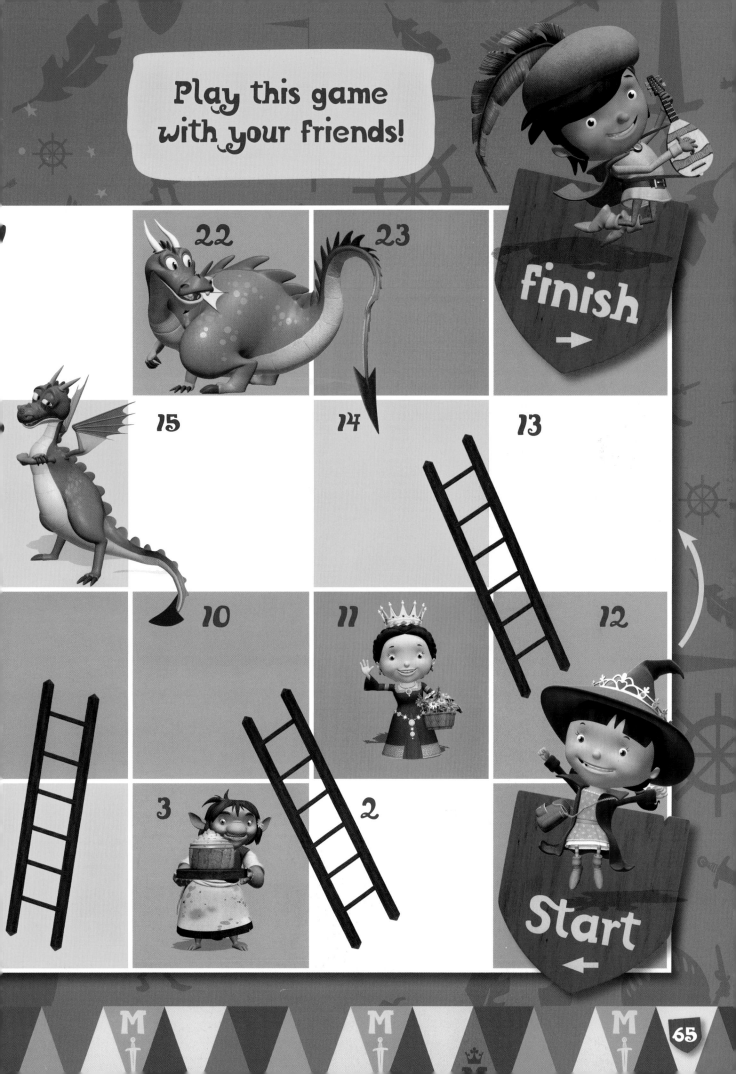

Play this game with your friends!

finish →

Start ←

22 23 14 13 15 10 11 12 3 2

65

The King sends Mike lots of postcards of his travels. This one shows the beast he just fought. Draw and colour in a scary monster in the postcard below.

Fernando's Farewell

Our tales of brave Mike have now come to an end
We must say farewell to our cheeky young friend.

From Sparkie and Squirt, and Evie and Mike,
Glendragon Village and the castle alike ...

Goodbye for now, but come back again soon.
We'll have more adventures, and I'll sing a nice tune!

Answers

Page 9: Mike needs his shield, sword and helmet.

Page 13:

Page 14: 1–e, 2–d, 3–a, 4–c, 5–b.

Page 15: Picture 3 is different. The feather is yellow.

Page 18:

Page 28: Sparkie can cook the bananas and pumpkins.

Page 31: Mike's helmet is pink, Sparkie's horns are flowers and Squirt's tail is a scrubbing brush.

Page 36:

Page 37:

Page 38: Piece b is missing.

Page 39: Mike needs to take path c.

Page 41:

Page 42: a–4, b–3, c–1, d–2.

Page 50: There are 19 pictures of Yip and Yap.

Page 51: Close-up c can't be found in the big picture.

It is time to be a Knight - and do it right!
By the King's crown!
MIKE
M